For Violet with love from Jeanne.

For Tessa & Sophie - H.C-B.

HODDER CHILDREN'S BOOKS

First published in Great Britain in 2017 by Hodder and Stoughton

A CIP catalogue record of this book
is available from the British Library.

ISBN: 978 1 444 91767 3
10 9 8 7 6 5 4 3 2 1

Printed and bound in China.

Hodder Children's Books
An imprint of
Hachette Children's Group
Part of Hodder and Stoughton
Carmelite House
50 Victoria Embankment
London, EC4Y 0DZ

An Hachette UK Company
www.hachette.co.uk
www.hachettechildrens.co.uk

*Hodder
Children's
Books*

TELL ME A STORY RORY

JEANNE WILLIS
HOLLY CLIFTON-BROWN

There was once a
lion who slept on
a little girl's bed.
The lion could
not sleep without
a bedtime story.

So every night the little girl told him one.

She told the lion
a bedtime story
about her first day
at nursery school.

She told the lion
a bedtime story
about when the
tooth fairy came...

...and the night her baby brother was born.

She told the lion a bedtime story every night - through a starlit summer, a misty autumn and a frosty winter.

Then one night,
in the spring,
the little girl wasn't
there any more.
Some say she grew too
big for her bed.

But others say
she grew too
big for her lion.

The lion really missed
the girl. And the stories.
How could he sleep
without them?

So the lion made up his own story, and he told it to himself. And it went like this:

There was once a girl who missed her lion.

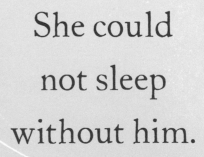

She could not sleep without him.

And as the missing grew and grew
she decided to go back and find him.

"Tell me a story, Rory,"
said the girl.

And the lion
(whose name was Rory)
did.

He told her a story about the
lion and the girl on the moon.

And a story about the girl and
the lion who went to sea.

And the one about the
girl who left her lion –
and then came back.
"This is our story," he said.

"Does it have a happy ending?"
asked the girl. And the lion said...

"Yes!"